What's So Special About Me?

I'M ONE OF A KIND

by Janet McDonnell
and Sandra Ziegler
illustrated by Joy Friedman

Created by
THE CHILD'S WORLD

Distributed by CHILDRENS PRESS®
Chicago, Illinois

CHILDRENS PRESS HARDCOVER EDITION
ISBN 0-516-05711-1

CHILDRENS PRESS PAPERBACK EDITION
ISBN 0-516-45711-X

Library of Congress Cataloging in Publication Data

McDonnell, Janet, 1962-
  What's so special about me? : I'm one of a kind / by Janet
McDonnell and Sandra Ziegler ; illustrated by Joy Friedman.
      p.   cm. — (What's so special)

    Summary: A girl nicknamed Anna Banana rejoices in all the ways she
is special and one of a kind, from the five orange freckles on her
nose to the way she giggles at her brother's jokes.
    ISBN 0-89565-419-9
    [1. Individuality—Fiction.]   I. Ziegler, Sandra, 1938-
II. Friedman, Joy, ill.   III. Title.   IV. Series.   88-2872
PZ7.M478436Wh   1988   CIP
[E]—dc 19   AC

1 2 3 4 5 6 7 8 9 10 11 12 R 96 95 94 93 92 91 90 89 88

What's So Special About Me?

I'M ONE OF A KIND

What's so special about me? Well, no
one else is exactly like me. I'm the
only me in the world. I don't know
anyone else with a name exactly like
mine — Anna Marie Carmichael.

My brother calls me Anna Banana. It
used to make me mad. But now I like
having a nickname — it makes me
different.

No one else looks just like me. Mom
says my hair is the very same color
as honey.

And Dad says my eyes are as blue
as the lake where we go fishing.

I'm the only person I know who has
exactly five orange freckles.

My brother says some day when I'm
sleeping, he will play "connect-the-dots"
on my nose to see what picture my
freckles make.

I have a special way of eating graham crackers. I like to bite them all around the edge and then dunk them in milk.

I also have a special bedroom. Dad
painted stars on the ceiling for me.
And I have all of my favorite things
on my shelves.

Sometimes I wish I could play baseball as well as my brother does.

But he wishes he could turn
cartwheels like I do. It takes a
lot of practice.

Sometimes I wish I could play piano
like Mom. She can make pretty music
whenever she wants to.

But I'm good at painting pictures. Mom
says my pictures turn our kitchen into
a rainbow.

I like colorful things. My favorite
shirt has different-colored hearts
all over it. And my favorite shoes
have rainbow-colored shoe laces.

I also like anything to do with
airplanes — I want to be a pilot
some day and fly my own airplane. It will say "Anna Banana"
on the tail wing.

When we go to the library, I check out airplane books. My brother checks out joke books.

He says he likes to tell me jokes
because I giggle so much. I like
to giggle. No one else has a
laugh that sounds just like mine.
Sometimes I laugh so much my
cheeks hurt.

I have a special secret hiding place.
I go there when I'm mad, or want to
be alone,

or when I want to pretend that I live
inside a tree.

And I have a very special friend —
my dinosaur. I named him Pokey.
I tell him my secrets and he keeps
them to himself.

All of these things make me special.
No one else anywhere is exactly
like me. I'm one of a kind.